Badge in the Shadows

Preston Olson

Published by Preston Olson, 2022.

BADGE IN THE SHADOWS

First edition. June 24, 2022.

ISBN: 979-8201318147

Written by Preston Olson.

Table of Contents

Prologue 1

Shadows Knock 2

Dressing The Dragon 11

A Spark and A Flare 20

Out of Room 26

Did You Knock? 34

An Old Fashioned Mixer 39

Long Winding Roads 46

Fire Burns Brighter After Midnight 52

Organized Chaos 59

What Now? 65

Epilogue 67

Afterword 68

In loving memory of my Father, Michael Carl Olson. You left behind a wonderful wife in my Mother LeAnn Olson. You raised two boys into men and your sacrifices are never forgotten. Your legacy lives through us and ours through you. Put in a good word to the "Big Guy" for us. Love, your Family.

Prologue

Detective Reisen is sailing toward his piece of mind. The sound of waves crashing against the shoreline echoes across Navy Pier. Leaving an everlasting impression on the sand. His vessel is a tribute to his passion for fishing and sailing across the Great Lakes. A boat may qualify as a luxurious asset. However, our everyday hero is far from a luxurious man.

He is a spiritual soul who believes the good will outweigh the bad in people. A blue-collar working man living out his American dream. Feels sanguine within his world.

When questioned by friends or loved ones, "How he was a single bachelor on the Chicago police force?" Detective Reisen has a response loaded like a criminal's gun. However, our wholesome lover boy believes he may have found his soul mate.

A woman regarded by the elites in Chicago as, "A breath of fresh air." Blonde with blue eyes and a full voluptuous figure. Boasting a smile that would stop a baby from crying.

The cornerstone of her beauty lies within her intuition, and uncanny ability to discover what others can't. A well-renowned reporter with major credentials.

Some folks squeak, "She attracts unwanted attention." Others say, "She has the kiss of death." Detective Reisen admires her passion and would rebuke the notion of anything less than the ladder. Bonnie Butterfield is more than a modern-day vixen. She is as good at capturing criminals as captivating an audience.

Shadows Knock

Awakened from a deep slumber by a powerful hammering sound, I sprawled out in bed as the pounding surmounts. Slowly rising to throw the covers off me. Treading forward while infuriating beating taunts me. Peering through a window as darkness consumes the sky. Who is knocking before the first break of sunlight?

My wall calendar marks today as Saturday, May fourth, 2024. Knocking resumes as I barrel for the door. Wiping cold from my eyes, the last thing I need is a surprise. Perhaps, a solicitor or door-to-door salesman. For heaven's sake, it's too early for the mailman!

Eye on the peep-hole unable to see who is on the other side. A shadow flickers into sight. "Good morning Detective Reisen!" a daunting figure booms.

In flesh and blood standing before me weathering a torrential downpour is Captain Davis; head of Progressive Task Force Twelve Z. Aging like vino in his early forties, broad-shouldered and smoking. A touch of gray glosses his wavy brown hair with a neck tougher than leather. My curiosity is reaching another level.

Captain Davis has been with the Chicago Police Department for twenty-three years. During his tenure, noble police officers have *resigned, found work elsewhere, or unfortunately fell* in the line of duty. Standing as a testament to perseverance. He is respected, admired, and admonished by his peers. Political elites gush over his charisma.

A cinch to lead Progressive Task Force Twelve Z upon its creation by Mayor Riley back in January. Sought after for political office; which he refuses each political season. Declining spotlight instead fulfilling deeper satisfaction in crime-busting. Coupled with utter annoyance from back-stabbing politicians. Captain Davis feels his purpose hasn't been served, but he serves admirably.

"Captain Davis? What a surprise! Please, step inside." Holding open the door as a good-faith gesture.

"Thank you for saving me from that wicked storm!" Davis amplifies.

We shake hands as he leaks everywhere. My radio faintly plays in the background.

"No trouble. Would you care for a cup of coffee?" I ask.

Hat in his hands, tapping his fingers along the brim. He seems nervous.

"Coffee? Absolutely! Coffee would be top-notch," Davis bellows.

"Hang your coat up and follow me." Stopping after a few paces. "Must have left the radio on from last night," I say, turning up the volume.

A weather meteorologist mentions, "Rain showers will continue."

Preparing coffee as Captain Davis continues our conversation, "Sorry to drop in on you unexpectedly."

From the corner of my eye, he appears distraught. "Save your apologies. You're always welcome here," I state.

"Thank you. Hardly see anyone on the road in this storm," Davis implies.

"Weather has taken a nasty turn," I reply anxiously.

"You wouldn't believe it. Fog is thicker than a fat sheep's wool!" Davis jokes.

"Ha-ha, clever!" I shout, grinning wide.

The mood lightens, awareness heightens, and my chest tightens.

"Thank you. Thought popped into my head on the way here. Anyhow, the reason I stopped by—"

Beep-Beep! Whoop! Chug! Crackle! Crunch! Whoosh!

We flinch as hot caffeinated liquid finishes brewing.

"Coffee is ready," I squelch, feeling massively awkward.

Captain Davis smiles. "Sure is!" he chuckles. Both his hands rest on the coffee maker. "Get a look at this contraption," Davis says. Shaking his head pouring himself a fresh cup.

A few big gulps help my anxiety plateau.

"Let me get down to brass tax. Would you happen to know a man named Luis Reinhart?" Davis inquires.

"Know him?" I ask feeling puzzled. "More than that. Luis and I served in the same unit during our tour of Afghanistan. When we last spoke Luis was having a fundraiser for his mayoral campaign," I detail.

Sipping coffee slowly, and bracing for what Captain Davis might say. "Your friend is extremely vocal," he relinquishes.

Surprised by his observation, halting before replying. "About what exactly?" I inquire.

Captain Davis sizes me up, taking a long sip before speaking. "Ridding corruption from within the city government."

"I was unaware, politics isn't my field of study. Do you mean Luis raised hairs on the back of a few necks?" I ask.

"Possibly, does he have any enemies?" Davis inquires.

"Not to the best of my knowledge. Luis Reinhart is an honorable man. Level with me; is he in danger?"

Captain Davis's face doesn't break while posturing up straighter than a pole, "Received a phone call last night from an untraceable number. A voice said, 'Keep Luis Reinhart's name out of the newspapers until after the special election or else.'"

Tangling with my inner thoughts, "Or else what?" I ask.

"Luis will be a dead man. Phone call disconnected before I uttered a word," Davis divulges.

Staggered as if a prizefighter's punch connected in my abdomen. "You must be kidding!" I shout. Jumping up running my hand through my hair in disbelief.

"I wish this was a sick joke. All of the details are troubling," Davis says crisply.

"This is a mess!" Kicking over a stool. "Luis wouldn't jeopardize this opportunity," I growl.

"Guess who the janitor will be?" Davis asks.

Stopping in my tracks and facing him.

"You deserve an opportunity to sort this mess out. Recognize the magnitude of each fact surrounding Luis's disappearance," Davis says sternly.

Head sitting sideways, cold numbing anxiety *piercing* my nerves. "What are you saying?" I ask.

"A man turned up dead on South Archer Street a few hours ago. Patrol found a body sticking out of an alleyway folded up like lunch meat. Did some quick research around the Twelfth Ward of Chicago where Luis Reinhart is Alderman. Unfortunately, Luis's fingerprints were lifted off the victim," Davis discloses.

Devastated as anguish *crashes* into me like two pillars collapsing on each other.

"Breaking bad news doesn't suit you," I acknowledge.

"Doesn't mean Luis killed him. Could have found him that way, maybe a struggle, or might be nothing," Davis insists.

"Sounds like more than nothing," I counter.

Captain Davis glances down then up at me, "Find Luis before time runs out for him and us," he decides.

Shell-shocked struggling as I pull my words out of the void, "... Who's the homicide victim?" I ask.

"John Marshall," he replies. "Age sixty-three, residence in Bridgeview, Illinois, and a Cook County Circuit Court Judge."

Unable to believe my ears. "When the news teams arrive I have even less time," I huff.

"I will hold a press briefing to announce Judge John Marshall's death on the afternoon news. We will have his autopsy expedited," Davis says.

"Did you check Luis's residence?" Sliding my Glock 27 pistol into its holster ready for departure.

"Nobody home—neighbors haven't seen anything unusual," Davis replies.

"Did you contact Luis's campaign headquarters?" I ask.

"Yes. Nothing good came of it."

Holding out hope for a shred of uplifting news. "What did they say?" I inquire.

"Luis Reinhart's lead campaign staffer said, 'This week's plans are on hold,'" Davis replies.

"Any particular reason? Is Luis dropping out of the race?"

"No. The reason provided was personal. I assume stress from the campaign trail."

"You assume or are you not ready to convict a man that appears guilty from every angle?" I ask out of frustration.

"Lay off Reisen!" Davis shouts. "I may select any officer with a hair up his behind to track down your friend," he scolds. "Think big picture; help pull Mayor Riley off our backs. You wouldn't be assigned this case if I didn't have *faith* in you," Davis barks. His face is hotter than a toaster oven on full blast.

Sensing I poked the bear one too many times. Reeling in my attitude knowing circumstances could be worse. "Knew a vacation wasn't in the cards. This should count as overtime," I emphasize.

"Are you in or out?" Davis asks.

Batting an eye at him. "Give me the case," I decide.

"We are both being dealt a bad hand. Go all in finding Luis," Davis implores.

"Sounds as if you're working the roulette wheel," I joke.

Scoffing at my remarks. "The special election is in three days," Davis scowls.

"I heard the great news. Don't expect a parade," I joke.

"Glad your humor hasn't left you. If we send out an all-points bulletin for Luis Reinhart his chances will go up in smoke. Word around the campfire is Mayor Riley, her challengers, and several aldermen will capitalize on any mistake we make," Davis grimaces.

"Seems as though someone will benefit from Luis disappearing," I insinuate.

Placing his hand on my shoulder, "Let's not give City Hall an excuse for slashing funds or the local news further reason to exploit us." Pushing his index finger into my chest, "Bottom-line Reisen, this is in your hands," Davis stresses.

Numerous scenarios of Alderman Luis Reinhart in danger flash across my mind. "I will find Luis!" I declare.

Captain Davis nods. "Oh, almost forgot to mention; Detective Dewalt will work alongside you." Passing me his phone number on a thin piece of paper with coordinates to the crime scene. "He's been notified of the situation. Fill him in on the details."

"If you insist." Wincing from the idea of having a partner.

"Detective Dewalt is inexperienced but he comes from good water," Davis reassures, attempting to soften the blow.

Partaking in a final sip of java. "I appreciate your hospitality. Do me a favor and keep your head on a swivel," Davis says winking.

Mustering up a cheeky grin, "I will. I'll be in touch soon."

We make haste for the exit. "I will adjust your vacation time in the system log," Davis acknowledges.

Reaching the door we shake hands. "Thank you. Depending on how this goes I may need time off," I admit.

Captain Davis starts leaving but abruptly turns around. Perhaps, something burning a hole in his mind. "As you may have heard," his voice grows louder as the distance between us increases, "there aren't any real heroes in this city anymore! Legends, tall tales, occasionally a feel-good story. Citizens of Chicago deserve a hero! Someone the kids can look up to! Someone who stands for them on top of his convictions!"

Before I make a sound Captain Davis disappears into the *eerie* morning fog.

When Captain Davis hired me a few months ago he said, "Serving the residents of Chicago is where we will make our impact felt." If I didn't share his sentiment this task force wouldn't exist but Alderman Luis Reinhart may not either.

Working alone is my preference. Nothing wrong with having a partner. Trust is a hard ticket to sell after grasping how easy selling out is. An associate creates a gallimaufry of complexities: an edge at making up lost time—on the flip side—another soul to worry about.

Pouring coffee into my thermos while gathering myself. Needing laser-focus—knowing if not—what it would cost. Checking my cell phone when another banging sound begins. Wishing I was fibbing feeding you lies out of my hand. Wishing this day would end!

Scanning the room; searching for what Captain Davis left behind. Not one of his parcels lay in sight. Making a beeline for the door. Today has turned into a mighty big chore.

"How are you sugar?" a soft voice asks. Graced by the presence of my dear lady friend, Bonnie Butterfield. She is elegant, witty, and a *blessing* in the flesh.

Luis Reinhart's misfortune has my prior arrangement escape my thoughts. "I will manage." Tightly caressing Bonnie against my chest. "A lot of ugly people in Chicago; nice to see someone beautiful," I say.

"I missed you!" Bonnie clamors. Laying a big kiss on my lips. How could I resist?

"Missed you more. I have bad and slightly worse news. Which would you prefer to hear first?" I ask.

"Darling no! I was afraid of this. Give me the ugly version." Holding me and gazing into my eyes.

"Vacation is on hold for a friend of old," I hint.

Twirling her long locks of blonde hair, "Nobody better for the job I suppose," Bonnie sighs.

"Nothing sneaks past you. Do you remember my friend Luis Reinhart?"

"Of course!" she jeers. "After you broke the news about us dating, Luis bought me that lovely pink sapphire necklace." We glance at her neck. "Funny, I'm wearing it now," Bonnie giggles.

"If that's not a coincidence I don't believe in them." We laugh and kiss. "Luis fancies himself a rather classic man. Performing kind gestures where he roams. I am afraid he attracted the wrong attention," I say.

"He must take after you," she says. Kissing me gently— scratching the back of my head.

"You are in a league of your own," I compliment. Tasting Bonnie's sweet lip gloss. "An unprecedented situation occurred," I say as her eyes widen. "Captain Davis informed me Luis is in danger," I confess.

"Dear, Lord! How can this be? This is terrible! How may I assist?" Bonnie asks hysterically. Her arms tremble as she clamps down on mine.

"Glad you asked," I reply. Pulling her close, "Your snooping skills are warranted."

"Do I have enough time?" Bonnie asks, frantically shoving her head into my chest.

"When we start odds will *shift* in our favor." Deeply kissing wishing time would freeze. "Scope out who is financing Luis's opposition and make yourself comfortable."

Her hand presses against my face, "Will you be okay?"

"We will be okay." Kissing her with all my might.

"I'm afraid of what could happen if you don't find Luis."

"Don't spend time being afraid. Help me find Luis," I say as we smooch. "Call me once you find anything. Slight details are key for cracking open Luis's disappearance."

"You have the one key you need," Bonnie confides in me.

Caught in her majestic gaze. Glowing dreamy eyes meet my hawkish glare. Locking lips as if this is the last time we will perform such an act. *Praying, I will return in one piece.*

Leaving the room when my heart beats for her, "You are the bright spot of my day," I say.

Bonnie's face lights up—eyes glistening. Slipping on my coat and hat. Grabbing my keys while clutching my thermos. Before she says another word I am history. Venturing into the city's dark side.

Dressing The Dragon

Fitted in the driver's seat of my fully-loaded blue Ford Mustang SVT Cobra R. Punching coordinates into my laptop. The area appears familiar. Perhaps, a clue if memory serves correctly.

Dialing Detective Dewalt's phone number. I am greeted by him chewing, "One moment," he muffles, placing me on hold. "More coffee please," Dewalt says.

"Hello, Dewalt. Are you there?" I ask.

"I am expecting you."

"I'm flattered. You must be working hard," I joke.

"In the preparation stage," Dewalt retorts. Slurping his coffee. "A morning ritual if you wish. Do you have one?"

"Mine was interrupted," I reply.

"What a drag, could ruin your day," Dewalt nags.

"Throw me a bone," I crow. "We must run this show like clockwork if we have any chance of saving Luis. Where can we meet?"

A brief pause induces intermittent static. "Meet me at Big Clark's Diner on Damon Street. Remember, I'm not on duty yet," Dewalt stammers, hanging up.

Engine roaring—wheels rolling *swiftly* over the pavement. Splashing puddles—breathing heavy—*praying Luis is breathing*. Rain is pounding as a strange feeling lurches over me. Hair standing up on my arms, captured by a feeling of being watched.

Big Clark's Diner grows in size as I approach. Maneuvering into a suitable parking spot. A few people are out taking a stroll; draped with umbrellas. Unable to shake a cold chill as I exit my vehicle.

Stained glass windows taper the front. An arching neon sign lit up in blue letters reads Big Clark's. A giant glazed doughnut spins overhead.

Entering inside a small chalkboard on wheels lists their specials. Detective Dewalt motions for me. Making my way to his booth—we shake hands—sitting across from each other. A spread of half-eaten french toast, orange juice, and coffee is in front of him.

"Are you nervous?" I ask gingerly.

Dewalt's eyebrow raises as he munches a big bite. "Nervous? Why would I be nervous? Everything I need is here." His sublime look of confusion is priceless.

"You're eating like you're going into battle for the last time," I mock.

Coughing—convulsing—he is hard-pressed not to laugh. "We have a case to solve. I need brain food," Dewalt retorts.

"Allow me to explain something about brain food—"

A waitress arrives without a second's notice. Her name tag reads Kimberly. A tall brunette her hair in a ponytail held by a multi-color butterfly clip. Decorated in turquoise beads, gripping a coffee pot. "What may I start you out with today?" she asks. Sliding a menu and a cup in front of me. "Our potato soup is delicious," Kimberly recommends.

"Coffee is all please and thank you, Kimberly."

"More coffee," she repeats. Smiling as she fills my cup.

She looks over at Dewalt, "May I get anything else for—"

"Check, please," he says, wiping his mouth with a napkin.

Kimberly nods and *rushes* away.

"Don't take this as being short. I'm steaming mad! We don't have an illustrious picture of Luis's disappearance."

"I concur. Do you believe Luis is hiding or was kidnapped?" Dewalt asks.

"Nobody has asked for ransom," I respond undecided.

"Perpetrators might not know who to ask," Dewalt theorizes, slurping coffee loudly.

"Possible conclusion, the grim picture is we may be chasing a corpse," I decry.

"What will someone gain from all of this?" Dewalt asks.

"Timing is odd at best. If Luis is narrowing in on winning a special election for mayor what nut case would go after him?" I ask.

"Highly suspect to your point. A fanatic's field day. Have you ever seen Luis Reinhart in action?" Dewalt inquires.

"Last time I saw Luis chance his luck was at a casino raising cash for a local charity. He is good with numbers."

"If you don't mind me asking, will you describe Luis?"

Focusing on Detective Dewalt, "Luis clamors passionately for fixing Chicago's finances. Making solid points along the way. We both come from outside of big city life. Raised on dirt roads in poverty. Our dreams were nightmares, and nightmares were our friends," I detail.

Silence befell across our booth and immediate area. Detective Dewalt's fingers tremble as he sips coffee. "Luis's gambling urge ... did he ever request money from you?"

"No. Perhaps, his finances have dwindled. Luis may have run into trouble with a loan shark," I suggest.

"Anyone good with numbers and finds luck in Chicago will draw attention," Dewalt says candidly. "When Captain Davis assigned me to the case, I ran a background check." Flipping open a silver briefcase layered in gold trim. "Luis Reinhart has a clean criminal record." Passing me a file folder.

"Someone stands to lose an awful lot or Luis hit rock bottom," I say. Flipping through the documents—stumped for clues.

"What are Luis's hobbies?" Dewalt asks.

"Eating Chinese food, golf, gambling, viewing art galleries," I list.

"Anywhere around this wonderful city?" Dewalt asks.

Ignoring his tone, "Luis brought me to a restaurant before. What sketches me out is the joint sits near the crime scene," I sneer.

"Thank you for the update. Who is the homicide victim?"

"Judge—"

"Wait!" Dewalt says, accidentally kneeing the table; shaking everything on top. "The homicide victim is a judge?"

"Yes. What's worse is Judge Marshall's death will be announced on the afternoon news," I dread.

"Lead the way partner," Dewalt replies.

"Are you on duty now?" I ask, knowing he is.

"Hope you brought a tip with your cheap humor."

Both of us stand as I leave a tip and Dewalt flips for the bill. Outside I observe a man cautiously driving. Peering my way with a menacing stare; eyes darker than onyx gemstones. Speeding off before I obtain a closer look. Left with a cold stillness inside me.

Nearly convinced a harbinger of death closed in on me, Detective Dewalt steps outside. Standing taller than me by a few inches and in good conditioning; as a good officer of the peace should be.

Withholding a secret from Detective Dewalt. When the time is right I will reveal how we paired. Truth be told I saw our partnership coming like a meteor over big sky country.

"Crime scene is west of here on South Archer Street. You can't miss it." Forgoing mentioning the creature passing by for fear of startling Detective Dewalt.

"Wait! Why are we taking separate vehicles?"

"Under present circumstances, the risk is elevated," I say begrudgingly.

"How so?" Dewalt asks pretentiously.

"For starters, driving in the same vehicle gives us away."

"Our appearance alone does that. I can drop my motorcycle off at home and ride with you," Dewalt interjects.

"If we drive separate vehicles we appear as two friends meeting for lunch," I contend.

"If someone told you I am a backseat driver they are lying," Dewalt insinuates.

"Ha-ha, we will drive together eventually. What happens if the car we are in becomes totaled? What if our tires get shot out?" I ask.

Detective Dewalt ponders my objectivity.

"You have to think of the problem beforehand," I imply.

He nods in agreement. "What if I get lost?" Dewalt asks.

"Do you want the address of the city morgue as well?"

"No. A landmark will suffice," Dewalt concedes.

"A giant puffy red dragon in front of the restaurant. You will see the dragon's head a few blocks back," I explain.

Detective Dewalt stands before me bewildered. Taking separate vehicles is a safety precaution deeply embedded in my brain's wiring. Heading for the crime scene feeling our plate spilling over the edge. Every fiber in me gravitates toward finding a driving force behind Luis's disappearance.

An uneven feeling grips my chest left with sharp shortness of breath. Are Luis Reinhart's misfortunes self-inflicted? Due to extenuating circumstances? Outside influences leaving him with no perpetual escape? Each possibility leaves an enormous sadness inside me.

High-rise apartments shield the crime scene. The dashboard clock reads 6:30 a.m. Two hours since receiving notice of Luis Reinhart's disappearance. Detective Dewalt parks near me. Our vehicles hug the curb as we slide out.

Moseying around as spectators instead of detectives. A police patrol car is stationed close by. A woman officer inside assuring nobody tampers with the crime scene. Yellow tape is fastened around the chalk outline. A mighty eyesore for the lone business owner less than one hundred yards up the road.

Spotting a man peeking at us, "We caught someone's attention!" I snap.

Detective Dewalt follows my eyes but only sees the man's shadow. Dewalt pulls a binder out of his briefcase with Luis's picture sticking out. We walk toward the mystery man.

"Here's the restaurant with a big red dragon out front," Dewalt says.

"Better yet; our first lead," I suggest.

Reaching large crimson cushion-covered doors. Not spotting any security cameras. A sign above reads The Dressing Dragon.

Entering inside an aroma of frankincense blasts us. Funky pictures litter the wall. Strolling toward the front desk noticing staff preparing food and a woman cleaning. She notices us from afar. Her name tag reads Cheng Li. Rocking glitter and gold fingernails paired with short black hair. A look of intent in her hazel-colored eyes.

"Hello, Cheng Li. We are from the Chicago Police Department representing Progressive Task Force Twelve Z. I am Detective Reisen and this is Detective Dewalt." Flashing my badge, "We are working on something important—"

"Me too," Cheng Li hisses, slamming a drawer in the cash register.

"Have you seen this man before?" Dewalt holds up a snapshot of Luis Reinhart.

"Give me a minute." Putting her cleaning supplies away. Cheng Li studies the photograph. "No, but maybe the owner has. Please, wait here," Cheng Li says.

She nearly departs when Detective Dewalt speaks up, "Take this with you." Passing her Luis's photograph. "Thank you, we will wait here," Dewalt says.

Cheng Li scurries away while Detective Dewalt and I sweat in place. Praying the owner saw Luis Reinhart recently. If we aren't blessed with a lead we are at a severe disadvantage.

After a few minutes, Cheng Li approaches with whom I presume to be the owner. Hit with a jolt of interest for he is the same man who was watching us. Face chiseled with age while gray hair laces the crown of his scalp. Slowly moving using a cane in one hand; eyes fixated on us.

"I am Rahn Han," he says, as we shake hands. "Cheng Li says you are searching for a man, is this true?" Han asks.

"Correct. Any information would be—"

"Is this him?" Rahn Han interrupts. Holding up Luis's picture.

"Yes, sir. His name is Luis Reinhart. We believe he's in trouble," I imply.

Rahn Han carefully examines the photograph. "I recognize him. He has dined here for many years."

Rahn Han's words draw a *ray of light* into a dark room.

"When was the last time you saw Luis?" I ask.

"Help me and then I will assist you," Han grins, wrinkles bulging through his skin.

Believing Rahn Han lost his marbles, "What are you suggesting?" I ask.

"I may be of assistance on your journey ... however, you scared off my customers! Business is slow! Buy something and I will repay you with my eyes!" Han shouts.

"If you impede our investigation we will bring you down to the police station," Dewalt barks, puffing his chest out.

"Hold on Dewalt," I say, extending my arm in front of him. "Do you have spicy egg rolls?" I ask.

Rahn Han cheeses, "We certainly carry spicy egg rolls for two hungry policemen!"

"We have a deal!" I declare. "Please, toss in a few fortune cookies for the road."

Rahn Han punches in our order and I pay. We step aside for future patrons while Cheng Li proceeds with her duties.

"Since I purchased some of your delicious morsels, will you kindly tell us what you witnessed last night?" I ask.

"Before closing, Luis picked up an order," Han states.

"What time?" Dewalt asks.

Strumming his razor-thin goatee hairs, "Shortly before 11:00 p.m.," Han replies.

Feeling close—pressing for answers, "Did you notice anything wrong with Luis?" I ask.

"Luis looked tired," Rahn Han reveals.

"Any strange people lingering around?" Dewalt asks.

Scratching his chin; lost in deep thought. "A car drove near him wanting his attention but Luis waved them off."

Rahn Han's statement *raises* our eyebrows.

"Them? You saw more than one person in the car?" Dewalt inquires.

"I saw an outline of two people in the front seats," Han describes.

"Did you catch a good look at the vehicle?" I ask.

"Not well enough. Dimly lit streetlights work when they want," Han crows.

"Only business left on this block," I clarify. "Do you have a security camera facing outside?" I ask.

"Sorry, no," Han grimaces. A *disappointing* response in a *difficult* situation.

"Do you have any other details to add?" I ask.

"Heard a loud noise shortly after but that is nothing new. When I opened today a policeman with wavy hair told me a man died down the street. Luis went the opposite way so I didn't think he was in danger," Han explains.

"Thank you for being patient," I say. Gathering enough courage to smile. "Would you be kind enough to sign a witness statement?" I ask.

Rahn Han hesitates, "... I suppose."

Detective Dewalt jots down Rahn Han's statement. Judge Marshall dying nearby means a coincidence is out of the question. Clearing Luis Reinhart's name is a complex task. Obtaining Rahn Han's statement will help rule Luis out as a prime suspect.

Someone is calling me—directing my footsteps—urging action! Swinging open the doors noticing the patrol car is amiss. A metallic jade-shaded jeep idles deep in the abyss.

Frozen in time, squinting ahead while a storm brews. Different from the *grotesque* mutant at Big Clark's Diner. Glasses with purple frames shield his eyes. Inching closer his long face fixated on me. Not budging or breaking eye contact as he speeds up. Although his eyes are covered, I know he feels my stare penetrating his rage.

Tires rub the curb as Detective Dewalt steps outside raising his firearm, "Reisen, look out!" he shouts, firing a shot.

Twisting the steering wheel—brakes squeal—the jeep races off.

"Whoa! He nearly obliterated you!" Dewalt blurts.

"Did your gun misfire?" I ask.

Detective Dewalt's face is perspiring. Rising from the tumble I took; a near-death experience averted. Cracking a wide-eyed smile.

"His windows are bulletproof," Dewalt replies. Helping wipe the dust off of me. "If you have a death wish aim higher than being run over."

"Needed a closer view; feels like a success," I say.

"You are wild!" Dewalt shouts. "Is your spirit animal a bulletproof monk?" he asks.

Brushing off his question, looking square at Detective Dewalt, "Called his bluff didn't I? If he wanted to kill us we wouldn't be standing."

Detective Dewalt flips up his hat scratching away. "We need backup," he blubbers.

"Done deal. Did you catch his license plate number?"

"You bet! Let's chase him down!" Dewalt shouts.

"If we chase him he might wind up dead. Radio in the license plate number; we will head him off," I decide.

Hustling over to Detective Dewalt's motorcycle. He relays the license plate number to dispatch. I don't believe my ears—the suspect's vehicle isn't registered.

A Spark and A Flare

We quietly sit puzzled. Uncertainty decaying our resolve at an immeasurable proportion.

"Maybe I missed a number or letter," Dewalt whines.

"You have the number right. No mistake about it," I reassure.

"Should we give dispatch his description?" Dewalt asks. Holding the police radio against his chest.

"Won't help. He's probably listening on a police scanner and will head into hiding. I have a hunch he circles back," I imply. Entertaining a *buried* thought, "I won't repeat myself."

"What's eating you?" Dewalt asks.

"Something is off, had this feeling ever since leaving home," I explain.

"I shouldn't have eaten in front of you," Dewalt pokes. "Do you believe someone is attempting to scare us away?"

"They attempted—they will again—until we find Luis." My words *stew* in Detective Dewalt's mind.

A somber expression dissolves from Dewalt's face, "The feeling is mutual. I noticed the driver outside Big Clark's Diner," he confesses.

Detective Dewalt's revelation provokes me, "Why didn't you say something then?" I ask.

"Didn't want to sound the alarm before the fire. Could be nothing but I know better," Dewalt points out.

"We didn't stress the *unknown*. Believing Luis is breathing comforts me. You must believe we will find Luis alive," I emphasize.

"Do you trust me?" Dewalt asks.

"What do you mean?"

"You didn't mention the *creep* driving by earlier," Dewalt quips.

"This is our first time working together. I can't take any chances until I know what I'm up against."

"What we're up against," Dewalt corrects. "I am watching your back, Reisen."

"Likewise," I respond. "Are you up for springing a trap?"

Detective Dewalt is caught off guard. "Yes I am," Dewalt dares.

"Catching whoever wants us out of the way is a solemn ticket to Luis," I persuade.

"If they are human," Dewalt squeaks.

"No ruling out anything after what we witnessed," I add.

Cheng Li *power walks* toward us. Detective Dewalt and I are baffled.

"Listen! I must tell you ... nothing important—at least I hope not." Cheng Li's complexion is bright and blushing.

Sensing she is embarrassed by not mentioning this earlier, "Thank you, for coming forward," I say.

"Before I leave at night, I always clean the parking lot. The trash people leave behind ... you wouldn't believe these filthy ingrates! A bunch of food was spilled last night," she says, pointing to the side of us. "I clean the mess by myself. I always clean by myself!" Cheng Li howls, growing fiery with each passing second.

"I hear you crystal clear. What made you walk over here?" I ask in the nicest tone available.

"Sorry for venting." Her complexion resembles a ghost pepper.

"You are doing wonderful. Please, continue explaining," I encourage.

"Anyway, an entire order of food was scattered there. Your friend's order was the same. I overheard him say, 'Hours had passed since he ate.' Nobody wastes food if they are starving," Cheng Li snorts.

Not exactly a break in the case but I appreciate Cheng Li's line of thinking while mulling over her claims.

Detective Dewalt tips his cap, "I thought you said you didn't see him," he growls.

"Not necessary Dewalt. Thank you, Cheng Li. Your contribution is appreciated," I advise.

"Sorry I didn't mention this earlier. My brother is a chef in the Dressing Dragon. If I mentioned this in front of the owner he would fire my brother! Please, do you understand?" Cheng Li pleads.

"We understand Cheng Li. Thank you for your cooperation," I reassure.

As Cheng Li walks away her remarks begin *sinking* in.

"We should compare notes," I suggest.

"Fine with me," Dewalt says from his vehicle.

"Luis is missing, Judge Marshall is dead, and then I meet with you; eating like it's your last meal!" I quip.

"We arrive at the crime scene. After questioning Rahn Han we know someone wanted Luis's attention," Dewalt adds.

"Correct," I say, delighted with his memory.

"We leave and I am almost splattered. The suspect's vehicle has never been registered. Cheng Li rushes over saying someone spilled an order of food. Maybe the person didn't like the food. Maybe Luis was in a struggle," I hypothesize.

"A starving man won't toss any food," Dewalt chimes in.

"Earlier you were chowing down like a dog without a bone. You might be an expert when food is involved," I joke.

He turns away in disgust. Tapping him on the shoulder. "One last thing I must know?" I ask.

Detective Dewalt looks back unnerved. "What?"

"When did that rotten patrol car leave?" I ask.

"Beats me. Darn shame. She could have chased down that maniac," Dewalt sighs.

Nodding in agreement—kicking pebbles in the gutter—weighing solutions against outcomes.

My cellphone begins ringing. In a mad dash to my car, I answer, "Hello, Bonnie! Please, speak glorious words."

"Allow me sugar. I miss you!" Bonnie exclaims.

Full of wonderment hearing her voice. "Thank the good Lord! You are a saint!"

"You are too sweet!" she bubbles. "I advise sitting down for this. Alderman Luis Reinhart was successful in reducing Mayor Riley's power in Chicago," Bonnie details.

Setting the phone on speaker mode, "What sort of power?" I inquire.

"Mayor Riley's spending power. Luis Reinhart secured enough votes to stop Mayor Riley's policies until her term expires. The special election is happening because Mayor Riley took over for the former mayor who resigned due to illness. Proponents of Luis Reinhart say the special election was inevitable because of how ineffective—"

"Are you saying Mayor Riley is involved in Luis's disappearance?" I cut in urgently.

"Can't be confirmed yet, sweetheart. Mayor Riley is being slaughtered in the latest polling data," Bonnie states in a ghastly tone.

Evidence of *political motivations* behind Luis Reinhart's disappearance mounts.

"We don't know if Luis was taken hostage or is laying low," Dewalt bellows.

"Or being hunted," I rebuttal.

We stare at each other—phone in my palm silent and calm. The feeling of being stuck drowns me.

"We need a helping hand but not from Captain Davis," I persuade.

"Why's that?" Dewalt asks.

"With what we know; Captain Davis is without a shadow of a doubt being watched by Mayor Riley. Her ilk may know Davis's whereabouts every second," I hum.

"Why is that an issue?" Dewalt asks.

"This morning Captain Davis visited my houseboat."

"Sounds fishy but what's our next move?" he speculates.

"This is where it gets complicated. We have a slim margin for error," I state.

"I follow you," Dewalt replies.

"If Mayor Riley is involved we must tread carefully or face being shut down before locating Luis," I divulge.

"How do we do that?" Dewalt asks.

"A friend outside of the department—"

"Can we trust him?" Dewalt interrupts.

"Yes. Good idea I touch base with him," I decide.

"A lot on the line ... this is heavy, Reisen," Dewalt says.

"We have no other option. His presence won't go unnoticed. By the time he arrives; we need a clear image of what we are up against," I declare.

All of us remain quiet—thoughts racing through my mind. Overcome with sick dampening emotion.

"Who is your friend sugar?" Bonnie squeaks.

Nearly forgetting she was listening, her voice *spoils* the darkness.

"Agent Martini. Met him at the police academy. Martini wasn't there long before I found out who he was," I say.

"What are you getting at?" Dewalt asks with disdain.

Sitting on the hood of my car. I reflect on how Agent Martini and I met, "Martini wasn't trying to become a police officer. He is an agent for the Criminal Intelligence Agency. A man nobody can touch; not Mayor Riley or any government agency besides his own."

"Why do you think he will help us?" Dewalt hisses.

"Worth a shot," I say shrugging. "Bonnie, you're a doll. Thank you, I will see you shortly."

"Alright, sugar. See you soon," Bonnie says, making a smooching sound before hanging up.

My nerves are a wreck. I won't speak for anyone else but the vibe is off. Tightening my wits before I throw a fit from siding with expedience over experience. As if the case were resting on a phone call.

Stretching my legs—punching in the digits on the keypad. The phone rings twice when a voice growls, "Hello, Reisen! Is this you? Is someone messing with me?"

"Martini, my friend, how are you?"

"I'm alive! Expecting you to pull up with Bonnie for the cruise. The tickets were outrageously priced!" Martini shouts.

"I know and I still haven't ruined the surprise for her. All I can tell you over the phone is a friend of mine went missing and if we don't find him I will be out of a job."

"Laying it on thick. If you can't find the fella how will I?"

"Martini you always did use your head. I will find him. What I need is insurance for when I do find him," I bark.

"Well, I owe you a favor. How may I assist?"

Breathing a sigh of relief, "I was hoping you would say that. I need you out here as soon as possible. I don't know how messy this will get."

"Tomorrow morning is the earliest I will arrive. Where do we meet?" Martini states.

"Rendezvous at Navy Pier," I say.

"Understood," Agent Martini replies, ending the call.

Out of Room

"Reisen!" Dewalt shouts, holding his side.

"What's going on?" I ask.

"My stomach is shaken up. I believe eating some Chinese food will heal me," Dewalt says nervously.

"You ate enough for a tiny village in Bermuda to survive on for a month an hour ago," I joke.

"Not funny! I am hurting!" Dewalt shouts.

"Here you are," I say. Pulling out a fortune cookie from the white paper sack.

Detective Dewalt points at my hand, "That tiny cookie won't help!"

"This isn't any ordinary cookie, this is a fortune cookie. Eaten after your meal; settling your stomach," I argue.

"The meal is in the bag. I hear it's bad luck to eat a fortune cookie before eating the meal," Dewalt whines.

"Knock yourself out." Passing Detective Dewalt the sack of Chinese food. "Don't forget to read the fortune cookie. A dose of enlightenment will help," I advise.

"Smart thinking!" Dewalt proclaims. Ripping one of the fortune cookies open. Popping it in his mouth—pulling out the thin piece of paper. Dewalt begins, "Every shadow has a pulse. Tread carefully or be reduced to pulp."

"Wow! Missed the mark in a big way!" I chorus.

"Has a nice ring to it," Dewalt mocks.

Behind on-time worry is *cemented* in my mind. "We—"

Before uttering another word the metallic jade-shaded jeep reappears. I don't believe my eyes. We made a mistake not pursuing or whomever this is made a mistake returning.

Creeping towards us slowly picking up steam. "Don't shoot!" I plead.

Detective Dewalt side-eyes me as if I'm a mad man, "What do you mean? We will be crushed!"

"He may be our only hope," I contend.

The jeep is full speed ahead and we are sitting ducks.

"Roll on my command! ... Roll!" I shout. Kicking up gravel as the jeep nearly impales Detective Dewalt.

"After him!" I snarl.

Detective Dewalt is in hot pursuit as I swing my car around.

Launching after the tires finish spinning. Picking up Detective Dewalt on the two-way radio as I gain ground, "How far are you behind him?" I ask.

"Not far behind. He's human; I see his outline," Dewalt insists.

"Don't head him off. Tail him!" I declare.

"What do you mean? I will catch this fool," Dewalt barks.

"No!" I shout. "We have to see if he leads us to Luis."

"Are you sure? I'm breathing down his neck!" Dewalt barks.

"Stay close and wait for me!" I decide while maneuvering through traffic.

Detective Dewalt and the phantom man possess a sizable lead. Vision becomes impaired as rain begins trickling down. Thunder roars over the dimly lit skyline. Lightning striking Lake Michigan in the distance. My lane offers more than a coming storm leaving me unsettled.

"He's pulling over," Dewalt alerts.

"Are you serious? Where at?" I ask.

"Union Station," Dewalt confirms.

"He will attempt to lose us. I'm still a bit behind. Wait for him to enter—then go after him," I direct.

"Once you have a man cornered his instincts will scream violence," Dewalt warns.

"Tread carefully. Don't draw unwanted attention. We must question him," I urge.

Closing in as I notice Detective Dewalt moshing inside after the suspect. Options for parking are slim. Breaking for the entrance—hustling down a flight of stairs. Slicing through lines like waves at a beach. Catching a glimpse of Dewalt sprinting after the suspect arises.

"Over here Reisen!" Dewalt hollers.

"Fantastic! There is only one way in and out of this restroom," I describe.

Detective Dewalt holds the door open, "Give yourself up! Make this easy on yourself," Dewalt orders.

"If you come in here I will put a bullet through you!" he screeches.

"No, you won't. Slide the gun over here and come have a chat," Dewalt rebuttals.

"No! No chat! No nothing! If you walk through that door consider yourself dead!" he challenges.

"Do you think you are a big man with a gun?" Dewalt asks

"What are you doing Dewalt?" I ask.

Detective Dewalt pats me on my shoulder, "I will throw my gun in there. If you are as bad as you say, meet me there and prove it."

"Are you insane?" I ask.

Raising his index finger to my lip, signaling for me to quiet down.

"Do you want a piece of me? You come in here and you come alone. I ain't afraid of you!" the suspect shouts.

"You should be afraid. Here I come," Dewalt grumbles, sliding his gun across the restroom floor.

Reaching my arm out to stop Detective Dewalt. "There are other alternatives," I whisper.

A futile attempt as Detective Dewalt sidesteps me. He enters and moves out of sight. I peek around the corner. Ready to draw my Glock 27 pistol at the sight of any foul play.

From the shadows, he charges Detective Dewalt. He throws a wild punch Dewalt catches returning with a swift kick in the man's lower abdomen; dropping him to a knee. Dewalt bulldozes him over as they collide. The suspect gains his second wind muscling Dewalt into a sink. Attempting a flurry of punches but Dewalt mostly evades connecting with a left hook in the man's ribs. They take a tumble to the ground and Dewalt lands on top. Dropping a few hammer fists on the suspect—he slides away—running wild.

Grinning as I wait for the right moment. He turns the corner and I spear him to the ground. "Ouch! I think my ribs are broken," the suspect cries.

Rolling him over and handcuffing him. Hoisting him to his feet. "Spectacular work!" I declare.

Detective Dewalt brushes himself off. Smiling wide as he approaches. A few marks are visible from the scuffle.

"Nothing wrong with a little roughhousing in good spirit, is there?" Dewalt asks.

"You won't get a complaint from me," I say.

"What's important is nobody was injured," Dewalt says.

"Not yet," I say.

Raising my eyebrow at the suspect pressed against the wall. His face is scarred from where you would normally see zits being popped. His eyes are bloodshot while sporting a flat haircut with three distinctive color streaks in red, silver, and black. Medium build, average height, and age around the late twenties or early thirties I assume.

"Do you have anything sharp that will prick or poke me?"

"My soul," the suspect replies.

Patting him down feeling nothing. "You lost fair and square," I growl.

"Doesn't change anything," he hisses.

"Your tough guy act won't hold up. What's your name?" I ask.

"Byron. Byron Maxwell. What's it to you swine?" Byron heckles.

"Don't waste our time. You are headed for the backseat of my car," I say.

"Where are we going?" Byron asks.

Tugging his shirt as we begin walking. Detective Dewalt follows close behind. "You are taking me to your boss!" I bark.

"Whoa! Are you groovy in the head? I won't take you anywhere," Byron whines.

Foot traffic is heavy. Onlookers pay close attention to us as we ascend the stairs. "You either work with us or I will guarantee this is your last ride," I stammer.

"If I help, will you cut me a break?" Byron asks.

"The choice is in your hands. Tell us who you work for," I say.

We reach the top of the stairs. Heading through the east doors of Union Station where I parked.

"I work for Masterclass. I don't know his real name," Byron whines.

Nearing my car. "Off to a great start! Keep talking," I say.

Detective Dewalt is in stride with us as a man sporting a black cowboy hat and beige raincoat stomps toward us. Black circle-rimmed shades sparkle in the sunlight which peeks through the passing storm. He sheds his raincoat and bolsters two pistols.

Detective Dewalt takes a bullet in the leg as we scramble. Ducking behind a parked vehicle. Returning fire at the active shooter. We melt the mad man with our bullets before he flees. Byron Maxwell lies dead on the sidewalk. Bullet holes layered through his chest from the assailant. Detective Dewalt slides down to the pavement favoring his leg.

The disturbance attracts a crowd. Paramedics respond to the scene. Bystanders gather around and fellow police officers rush to secure the area.

Leaning down applying pressure on Dewalt's leg while motioning for medical assistance. "Here comes help," I say. Pressing down on the bullet wound with my ripped shirt. Doing my best to stop the bleeding.

"Punk nailed me. Feels like the bullet went straight through," Dewalt groans in agony.

"You one-upped him. That maniac is gone for good. Focus on me—relax your breathing—the paramedics are here," I say.

Paramedics situate Detective Dewalt in the ambulance as I step aside in pure disbelief. Stepping over and patting the deceased gunman down; feeling nothing.

"If something happens to me I need you to know something," Dewalt grimaces.

"You will be—"

"I am a sibling of four," Dewalt begins, as his complexion worsens. "Growing up my three older sisters looked out for me but I protected them. When guys would come around selling drugs a few friends would help run them off," he coughs. "My past shaped me to become a police officer. I still live in that same neighborhood. Every morning the kids pass by and call me, 'Mr. Big Shot' as they head to school."

We laugh as I wipe away tears.

"I walk around with a lot of pride but I am proud to be your partner. Honored you gave me a chance," Dewalt finishes. Our arms meet as we shake hands.

"You will have another chance. I will ride with you and return here," I say.

"Don't be a fool! We don't have that sort of time," Dewalt growls.

"Are you sure?" I ask.

"Positive. Someone has to explain this to Captain Davis," Dewalt snickers. Writhing in pain—pointing behind me as the paramedics have him flush in the ambulance preparing to depart.

"Which hospital are you taking him to?" I bark.

A paramedic shouts, "Loyola!"

Ambulance doors close—and Detective Dewalt is gone.

Speak of the devil, Captain Davis is present. "So much for keeping quiet Reisen!" Davis blurts. Approaching with a somber expression on his face.

"I'm sorry. We were ambushed," I say, exasperated.

Captain Davis scans the scene—having a gander at the ambulance departing with Detective Dewalt inside. "By the look of things you had the jump on them. Will Dewalt be alright?"

"Detective Dewalt was shot in the leg. We *believe* the bullet went straight through," I say.

"I will be praying for him and arrange for his motorcycle to be towed home," Davis offers.

"Sounds wonderful. I will take his briefcase and duffel bag up to the hospital," I say.

"No objections here. Fella you had handcuffed is dead. What's that about?" Davis inquires.

"Lunatic opened fire on us. The guy we detained was the first one he shot before we took cover," I reply.

"Why did you detain him?" Davis asks.

"He tried running us down and was our lead suspect," I say.

"This shortens our time. Other departments hold back information until the investigation is complete. We don't have that luxury. Are we clear?" Davis, asks.

"Crystal clear," I respond.

"Who killed the shooter?" Davis asks.

"We both did," I confess. "With all due respect, I believe we need a police officer protecting Detective Dewalt's room tonight," I suggest.

"Can't afford to spare any manpower," Davis retorts.

"Real shocker," I huff.

"Will this impede your investigation beyond reprieve?" Davis inquiries.

"No. I am ready to proceed," I growl.

Captain Davis looks me over carefully, "I don't want you seen around here. I am taking over this crime scene. Your statement and concerns are duly noted. You have until tomorrow's evening news to find Alderman Reinhart," Davis declares.

Local news vans begin rolling up. A helicopter appears.

"I will find Luis before then. Dig up everything you can about the two deceased conspirators," I urge.

Gathering Detective Dewalt's belongings and setting them in my backseat. Refusing to look over my shoulder as my heart turns colder.

Did You Knock?

An aroma of black ice stemming from my air freshener overpowers my thought process. Peering in the rear-view mirror at myself with a focused glance. Every move is one step away from being set ablaze.

Nearing the boating docks where I wish to speak with someone who knows me better than myself. Stepping out of my car while raindrops coat the paint. Something feels off; reminding myself not to fret.

At my door sliding in the key. Turning the knob I don't hear the latch unlock. Drawing my Glock as I step past the grandfather clock.

"Bonnie! Bonnie Are you here?" I howl.

Proceeding up the stairs—receiving no response. A shadow lies outside the sliding doors. The time for games is over as I burst outside. Someone sits in a beach chair with their back turned.

Stepping ahead I notice the individual wearing a black bucket hat, orange shirt, and white sneakers. Legs crossed lounging in the cool breeze. "Who are you? Where is Bonnie?" I ask.

"Don't take another step!" the voice rumbles.

I feel something cold press against my neck. A familiar touch. Could it be her? I grab an arm turning around in one fell swoop.

Bonnie Butterfield holds a drink in both hands spilling a little on my arm. A bright glowing smile on her face. Facing back the other way—none other than Agent Martini himself stands grinning with his arms folded.

"You should have seen the look on your face!" Bonnie says as we begin laughing.

"We watched you pull in the parking lot and set you up to perfection. You must admit we fooled you," Martini jokes.

"I never should have introduced you both." Shaking my head. "Martini, you always were the king of pranks. Come here, you knucklehead!" I emphasize. Embracing each other as good friends should.

"How did you find me?" I ask.

"You seriously have to ask?" Martini inquires.

"No. You're good at what you do." I reply.

Pulling Bonnie close clasping the fresh glass of lemonade from her hand and passionately kissing her; a true love fest is born.

Regrettably parched as I take a sip. "Thank you, for the lemonade," I say, kissing Bonnie. "Listen—"

"You're welcome. What's going on dear?" Bonnie asks.

"We were ambushed," I sputter.

Bonnie wraps her arms around me; emulating a starving python. "Oh my gosh! I can't *believe* how fast this is escalating!" she says, sobbing on my chest.

"Everything will be gorgeous. Agent Martini is here to assist," I whisper in her ear. Attempting to soothe her *shattered* nerves.

"My apologies," Martini says. "Wouldn't have pulled this stunt—"

"You didn't know. I won't hold it against you. Added levity to my rotten day," I interject.

"Dewalt! Where is Dewalt?" Bonnie asks, gripping my arm and digging into my skin.

"Relax," I say, caressing Bonnie's head. "Dewalt was shot in the leg but is in stable condition at the hospital," I say feeling sick inside.

"What happened?" Bonnie shrieks.

"Had a suspect in custody at Union Station. A deranged gunman opened fire on us shortly after," I say as Bonnie gasps.

Martini grimaces staring at the ground and then up at me, "That's terrible," he replies.

"The gunman must have been waiting for us. I'm becoming certain as time passes," I say when a *striking* contrast dawns on me. Both vigilantes may have been working together unknowingly or uncoordinated.

Hit with a flashback from when the gunman began shooting. Lighting a fire under me, I reach for my phone. Holding up my index finger signaling for a brief silence.

Dialing Captain Davis's number. After two rings I hear *muffled* sounds.

"Hello, Captain Davis. Are you there?" I ask.

"Yes. What is happening?" Davis inquires.

"The gunman was wearing a black cowboy hat. Has the hat been checked into evidence?" I ask anxiously.

"There is a black cowboy hat on the ground tagged for evidence. What's the hat signify?" Davis inquires.

"Could be a break in the case. Are you able to get an identification on the shooter?" I ask.

"Don't count on it soon, bullets did a number on his face," Davis replies.

"What a shame. On my way to collect the hat," I say.

"I am rolling out. An Officer Ramona will have the hat at Cobbler Park," Davis decides.

"Be there shortly." Ending the phone call.

Returning my attention to Bonnie Butterfield and Agent Martini.

"What was that about, sugar?" Bonnie asks, embracing me and laying her head on my chest.

"A eureka moment. Had to call Captain Davis to make sure I wasn't going crazy," I reply.

Meeting her gaze and kissing her. "What's the verdict?" Bonnie asks.

"Jury is still out but I have a clue to guide me," I retort, smiling wide, laying a smooch on Bonnie.

Agent Martini slides the door shut behind him while holding a freshly mixed drink. "Reisen this place is amazing!"

"Glad you appreciate the finer things in life," I joke.

"Glad you have them. What did your friend say?"

"A police officer is holding evidence for me," I respond. "Bonnie, have you uncovered any link between Mayor Riley's involvement in Luis Reinhart's disappearance?" I ask.

"Not in that order. I turned over a few stones and Alderman Reinhart has stifled any major political achievement from landing in Mayor Riley's hands. His latest move was outlining a strategy to limit future mayoral control on city spending," Bonnie details.

"What a blow to Mayor Riley's ego!" Martini heckles.

"Not enough for contemplating kidnapping or murder," I reaffirm.

"You are right sugar but Mayor Riley's city budget is diabolical." Placing both index fingers against her cranium mimicking horns. "If she wins reelection her plan goes into effect without a majority of alderman support," Bonnie says.

My eyes widen, "Please, continue explaining," I say.

"An individual voiced his opposition against Alderman Reinhart's latest plan loudly. Made the front page of the newspaper this week," Bonnie details.

Handing me an article bookmarked on her cell phone. The headline reads "Prominent City Figure Worries About Losing Figures" by Isabel Radcliff. "Jake Frunk is an architect and philanthropist from Chicago's north side who believes he is being *targeted* by Mayoral Candidate Luis Reinhart's limited spending plan. Removing subsidies for art galleries owned by Frunk, among various cuts in city spending," I read aloud.

"We have a person of interest," I say.

Passing the article to Agent Martini and intensely hugging Bonnie. "Good work, love," I say, kissing her tenderly.

"We have our marching orders," Agent Martini states, passing back the cell phone.

"Time to gather the evidence but we don't have time to track down Jake Frunk yet," I say.

Bonnie stares at me leaning in with a smooch. Feeling every emotion rush through my veins and then nothing as our lips disconnect. "I miss you already," she says.

Always tough leaving Bonnie's side. Agent Martini says his goodbyes. Passing through the doorway—the idea of driving separate cars makes for a comfortable ride.

Reaching my car door. "Follow me," I say.

Agent Martini nods in agreement.

An Old Fashioned Mixer

Wind pressing against my vehicle as I drive. Changing lanes and not hitting any red lights along the route. In my rear-view mirror, I see Agent Martini a car length behind. Slowly pulling into state-of-the-art Cobbler Park. Hair standing up on my neck.

The sun is fading fast as I notice a police officer motioning for me. I drive up to her and roll down my window. Her badge reads Officer Ramona.

"Are you Detective Reisen?" she asks.

"Correct!" Flashing my badge, "Nice to meet you," I reply.

"Pleasure to meet you. Please, wait here." She fetches the black cowboy hat. "I'm Officer Ramona. Captain Davis was in a rush. He mentioned what your vehicle looks like to make sure you receive this hat." She hands over the evidence.

"Thank you, Ramona. Take care of yourself," I say.

With the evidence in my possession, I study it. The hat is unique. A leather band wrapped around the brim with gold clips holding it in place. The texture feels smooth with no tag. A closer look reveals a small branding on the inside, in three silver letters, reads RLG. A designer brand with one shop in all of Chicago. I know on the account of my grandfather loving anything they produced.

"Look out!" Agent Martini shouts.

I look up and Officer Ramona has the barrel of her gun facing down my skull. A shot is fired.

Agent Martini tiptoes to my window. I step out of my vehicle. Both of us peer at the deceased woman. A bloodstream mixed with rainwater runs into the sewage drain. Rain beats us profusely as we look on.

Agent Martini searches Officer Ramona.

"Thank you," I say.

"You would have done the same for me," Martini says.

Looking at the *lifeless* body of Officer Ramona.

"Have a gander at this," Martini says.

I reach down and swipe what Agent Martini is marveling at in his palm. Officer Ramona's badge is fake; made of some weird substance. Officer Ramona is no officer of the peace. Each thought swells in my mind at the notion Ramona was posing as a police officer to kill me.

Reaching for my cell phone to call Captain Davis. Met with a dial tone. Dialing an ambulance while Agent Martini checks out Ramona's car.

Sliding in my vehicle when Agent Martini approaches, "No phone or wallet. Ramona's weapon is a revolver with the serial number shaved-off," Martini describes.

"Oh, that reminds me, you killed her—your responsibility!" I declare.

Agent Martini rattles his head, "Fancy clue you have there. You almost took a bullet for it," he scoffs.

"Are you scared of paperwork?" I ask.

"Your jurisdiction; your paperwork," Martini rebukes.

"Fine. I will check the gun into evidence and fill out the report," I crow.

The ambulance arrives to take away Ramona's corpse. Agent Martini and I secure barricade tape around the scene.

"This hat is our lead. We must hurry or I won't be able to speak with the shopkeeper who sold this hat," I say.

"After you," Martini says. Passing me Ramona's gun.

Pulling out a bag from my center console and dropping it inside. Sliding the bag into the glove box and locking it.

Passing block after block to reach RLG's storefront. Years have passed since I stepped foot inside. Wondering if the owner is the same man who sold my grandfather his last pair of boots in 1998.

Pulling up and parking against the curb. Feels inevitable the weather will remain wicked. Opening my car door as the wind whips me onto the street. Firmly planted on the ground, Agent Martini meets me halfway to the entrance. A shadow dances in the light to a smooth jazz tune. Rubbing my eyes—the neon sign blinks open for business.

The inside hasn't changed much. Stepping on hardwood floors and noticing handcrafted merchandise line the walls. Agent Martini seems impressed; darting off to browse the merchandise. I head for the counter.

"Shalom!" A voice bellows.

"Good evening, and peace be with you" I reply.

Showing my badge to the man while placing the hat in front of him. "I am Detective Reisen. Agent Martini is browsing your showcase."

Having a clear look at him under the circular hanging light. Bolstering choppy gray hair on his mostly wrinkled face. A crimson-colored beard and thick bushy eyebrows with bits of gray fuzz layered throughout.

"Nice to meet you! I'm Matthew!" he booms, as we shake hands.

"Do you remember who you sold this hat to?" I ask, scooting the hat near him.

Pushing the hat back toward me, "Your Ralph's grandson aren't you?" Matthew asks.

Blown back by Matthew's question. "Yes, I am."

Matthew's face lights up like Christmas lights around a house. "Well, I'll be a horse's rear-end. You must take your looks from your mother's side. A shame you waited this long to visit," he says.

"Circumstances usually define my destination," I reply.

"Ha-ha! I understand your position. Ralph nearly spent more time here than me if he didn't have a beat to work."

"I was hoping you would be here," I encourage.

"Not when you see these prices. Taxes are killing my business. Raised the cost of everything to account for inflation. Not to mention the outrageous lease I have for this godforsaken storefront!" Matthew howls.

"Did you speak with anyone at City Hall?" I ask.

"City Hall? More like a mess hall!" Matthew jokes. "Spoke with Mayor Riley two months ago; she brushed me off. Some fella did pop in not long after; wants this area to be business-friendly," he heckles.

"You have a legitimate gripe and my sympathy," I persuade.

"Thank you. Your grandfather Ralph would be proud of the man you've become," Matthew states.

"I'm flattered. Do you remember the name of the fella that popped in here?" I ask.

"Let me see ..." Snapping his fingers, "He was Alderman Luis Reinhart!" Pointing his ring finger to the ceiling, "If I remember correctly he is running for mayor in the special election," Matthew reflects.

"You are on a roll," I joke.

"I don't trust what comes out of a politician's mouth nowadays. However, if this business savvy Alderman Reinhart will lower taxes and keep me above water then he has my vote," Matthew choruses.

"I appreciate your thoughtfulness. Luis will loathe your enthusiasm."

"You asked about the hat ... when you age you become wiser but you also get carried away," he coaxes. Matthew rotates the hat. "Lucky for you I keep a log of who buys merchandise for custom fitting purposes."

Matthew moves to the back room. He returns with a massive silver binder stacked full of pages held together by chrome spirals. Spread out across his workbench as he flips through tabs.

"Hallelujah!" Matthew cheers. "A gentleman named Canova purchased this hat custom fitted. Sorry, I don't have a last name for you. They aren't required to give one."

"I appreciate the information. Do you remember anything about Canova's appearance?"

"No. As a consolation, how about a goodwill offer of a hefty discount on any item on the shelves?"

Agent Martini appears from the shadows laying a handful of items across the counter.

"Allow me to introduce you to Agent Martini," I say as they exchange pleasantries. "Agent Martini is a terrific friend. Make good on your kind gesture by providing him with a whopping discount," I suggest.

"Done deal!" Matthew booms. "I will have your total due in a few minutes."

Matthew grabs a decorated belt buckle Agent Martini picked out. Fixating his glasses on the item. Punching in the price—*the old-fashioned way*.

Moving outside taking in the crisp air. Closing my eyes, breathing slowly. Agent Martini joins me. "Don't let anybody say you aren't a good man. That discount made a gigantic difference," Martini beams. Loading his suburban with the designer bags from RLG.

"A small reward for helping me in a pinch. Matthew, from RLG, dropped a name," I gloat.

Agent Martini's head spins around, "Out with it!"

"He said, 'Canova was his name.' No last name," I reply.

"The name he gave was Canova?" Martini asks stunned. Stepping back, "That can't be right," he decries.

"What do you mean? You think Matthew is lying?"

"Not at all. A few months ago someone sent an anonymous tip to our agency about a firearms smuggler."

"Do tell," I encourage.

"High-powered sniper rifles, machine guns, and mass quantities of dynamite. I am tasked with tracking down who is responsible."

"Have any luck?"

"After a recent interrogation, an individual confessed, 'their syndicate leader's name is Canova.'"

My jaw drops, "Appears as if the gunman was Canova, and your culprit is in a body bag," I state.

"Thank you for the vote of confidence."

"Always a pleasure working with you. What happened after the informant cooperated?" I ask.

"Routine procedure until the politics became messy."

Martini waves his hands and *mimics* a fire being doused.

"What do you mean messy?"

"Diplomacy is a roadblock or an off-ramp for criminals."

"Never heard of you being unable to clear a path," I scoff.

"You have more zingers than Hostess Brands," he jokes. "The informant's defense team reached a deal with the prosecution."

"Justice system working out the kinks as usual," I say.

"Every human is entitled to their opinion," he smirks.

"Where is this shadow man?" I inquire.

"Zenith is the name of the informant. He was exiled under conditions that he would never return to America. Turns out Canova is from the same Island as Zenith ... was from the same island."

"This Canova character is out walking scot-free and almost kills Dewalt and me! Why weren't you or anybody else able to locate him?"

"He was in hiding. His country doesn't honor extradition laws. If this is the same Canova, we are up against a shadow militia."

Tapping my foot on the ground as rain falls harder. Detective Dewalt's condition crosses my mind. From what I gather, Canova's henchmen may be coming to finish the job.

"I have to visit a friend. Are you coming?" I inquire.

Agent Martini raises an eyebrow glancing in my direction, "What do you mean? Am I the odd man out here?"

Sensing deep undertones of sarcasm I ignore Agent Martini's questions while gleaming with confidence and heading for my car. "Follow close behind!" I holler.

"Wait! I am starving," Martini says.

He jogs over to a food truck nearby. Easing over I notice a lemon shake-up with a Chicago-style hot dog in his hands. The vendor is a husky fella with a black goatee, square-rimmed glasses, and curly brown hair. His name tag reads Spencer.

"How about those Chicago Bulls?" Spencer asks.

"They have a chance to win the NBA Finals this season," I declare.

"They are good but they aren't gelling the same way Miami is," Spencer counters.

Laughing as I focus on Agent Martini. Contemplating how to premise my statement.

"Something is weighing heavy on my mind," I begin. "One way or another I will find out who is behind this. A shadow always reveals itself," I finish.

Agent Martini nods while biting off his hot dog as we click our cups together. "Cheers!" he shouts.

Sipping my beverage and *praying, that Luis Reinhart's last breath wouldn't occur as I take a breather.*

Long Winding Roads

Night falls rapidly on a day that began with no end in sight. Traffic turns monotonous as Chicago's nightlife picks up steam. Mind-boggling how trouble pursues us—justice fleeting into a shadow of doom—vacuum sealing our fate.

Reliving magnitudes of scenes: nearly being rundown, Detective Dewalt taking a bullet in the leg, and Agent Martini saving me from certain demise. Each bit swirling around in my inner thoughts. Part of the job—part of me.

Agent Martini trails me as we inconspicuously roll into the hospital parking lot. Parking a few car lengths down from the emergency doors.

Gliding toward Agent Martini. "Wait here in case something happens," I order.

"I will start that report for you," Martini replies.

Brushing Agent Martini's statement off as a snide remark. Grabbing Detective Dewalt's duffel bag. Marching toward the hospital doors.

Heading to the patient registration center. A woman with bright red messy hair is behind the desk. Her name tag reads Jane. Phone in her hands as she looks up giving me the stink eye.

"Hello I am looking for a patient," I say.

Jane sets down the phone, "Uh, hello! Your looking for a patient and don't know where they are?"

"Sorry to trouble you. His name is Jim Dewalt and he's expecting me. Will you please call his room?" I ask.

"Not how it works!" Jane scowls.

"How does it work?" I ask.

"Sign this!" Passing me a visitor sheet on a clipboard. Signing the sheet as Jane pulls it from me. Tossing a visitor pass at me, "Take this!" she demands. "One Moment," Jane says to the person on the phone; placing them on hold. "Who is the patient?"

"Jim Dewalt," I say.

"Sure. What's your name?" Jane inquires.

"Detective Reisen." Flashing her my badge.

"Oh." Jane's expression comes apart as she begins sweating. Tapping buttons on the keyboard in front of her. Searching for Detective Dewalt in the computer system.

Jane picks up the phone pressing buttons on the keypad, "Hello, Mr. Dewalt?"

Hearing a muffled voice over the phone from where I stand.

"Great! A Detective Reisen is here to see you. Are you seeing visitors?" Jane inquires.

Hearing another muffled voice. "Okay I will send him up," she says, hanging up the phone. "He is in a private room numbered three hundred twenty-eight on the third floor."

"Thank you, Jane."

"No trouble, Detective Reisen."

Moshing toward the elevator doors as a cool sensation encases me. Pressing the button in on the elevator panel. A brief delay before stepping onto the 3rd floor.

Shuffling down the hall lined with pictures of hospital board trustees. A man in a red sweatshirt and black skull cap peers around similar to a globe spinning in front of a classroom. Arms in his pouch like a kangaroo. Idling a distance ahead—speeding up at the sight of me. Looking for room three hundred twenty-eight and maybe he is as well.

Not a straight shot instead a solid haul. Catching a glimpse of a shadow entering Detective Dewalt's room. Bursting through the door feeling Dewalt could be a goner.

The evildoer's weapon is drawn on Dewalt as I charge him. A clicking sound ... his gun is jammed. Spearing him and he hits the ground wheezing. Knocking the weapon away and laying a big elbow to his cranium. Locking horns with the ornery and fiery delinquent. After a subtle tussle, the demon slips away.

On my feet fixing my clothes. Grabbing the bed railing while catching my breath. "How are you, Dewalt?"

"Better than I prayed for. We are getting out of here."

"What do you mean?"

"You heard me! I'm not waiting around for another whack job to come and finish me off!" Dewalt shouts.

"Please, be rational," I plead.

"I did all the rationalizing for you," Dewalt decides.

Detaching himself from the medical equipment. Reaching for his crutches and hobbling toward the door.

Jumping in front of Detective Dewalt, "One moment. We can't just go barging out of here. Ring for the nurse. I have a friend downstairs I must call."

"Fine! Did you at least bring me a change of clothes?"

Tossing Dewalt his duffel bag which rolled into the corner of the room. "Here's your outfit on the go."

Detective Dewalt heads for the restroom. Reaching for my cell phone dialing Agent Martini's number.

Martini answers quickly, "Man in a red-hood blasted out of the doors. Is that what you're calling about?"

"Your eyes are working. Follow him!"

"I'm all over him," Martini replies.

Hanging up the phone focusing my efforts back on Detective Dewalt who is sitting on the bed. The nurse enters the room. Unbothered by the shadow man; quite possibly not noticing. Her name tag reads Violet. Her hair is straight and black with big brown eyes on her round face.

"I see you are up," Violet says.

"I am getting the heck out of here. Here is my chaperon," Dewalt states.

"We strongly recommend against leaving in your present condition. You haven't even been here a full night," Violet contests.

"Thank you for your kindness. I gave you my insurance. Goodbye," Dewalt says. Taking his crutches in both arms swinging out the door and heading down the hall.

I tip my cap to Violet and trail Detective Dewalt. Reaching the elevator; pressing the button for the first floor. Dewalt has a look of misery on his face.

"Are you going to drive yourself?" I ask.

"Very funny. I may drive myself. I have a stinking license."

"How long do you need crutches?"

"Six months ... if everything heals properly," he grimaces.

"Depends how careful you are."

"Great positive reinforcement. I will roll faster next time."

"I was worried about you."

"I know," Dewalt seethes.

"How do you know?"

"The way you speared the hooded vermin trying to kill me; that is a friend spear. You don't nail a guy that hard for anybody," Dewalt jokes.

Laughing as we head for my vehicle. Agent Martini is calling my cell phone as I slide into the driver's seat. "Drive ten minutes north of Oak Street and on the left shoulder before the interstate there is a detour. Come take a gander at what I discovered," Martini claims.

"On my way," I reply.

Music puts ambiance in the air as we cruise. "Won't take long," I announce.

After a few turns, we are on a dirt path. I notice Agent Martini's suburban and pull up beside him.

"Over here!" Martini says, motioning for us.

Stepping out of the vehicle for a better look. Detective Dewalt and Agent Martini exchange pleasantries. Within arms reach of Agent Martini he points down over the cliffs. A compound with fishing docks expanding outward lies in the rolling fog. Boats wade with gear inside. Off the beaten path, we've reeled in a devastating catch.

"The perpetrator led me here," Martini reveals.

"This is a major development," Dewalt insists.

Observing the obstacle below as I am captured by enthusiastic enlightening emotion. Watching workers empty trucks assisted by spotlights.

"Our scope on the matter at hand has changed," I say.

"What do you mean?" Dewalt asks.

"How do you mean?" Martini inquires.

"We can't prance into a majestic compound," I scoff.

"Time to get Captain Davis involved," Dewalt suggests.

"Without backup? Those sliding gates are huge! We will be trapped inside before help arrives," Martini insinuates.

"Captain Davis hasn't failed us. Call him and formulate our plan!" Dewalt demands.

"Let's not bring too much heat down on this place otherwise we are liable to get shipwrecked," I plead.

"We need to bust in that rickety old boat dock tonight! Earlier you said, 'no waiting around,'" Dewalt jeers.

"Plans are fluid and looks are deceiving," I say. Soaking in the surrounding scenery. "Housing units with windows to shoot out of. Automatic lights all around—"

"What is your angle?" Martini interjects.

"If we blast inside unannounced we are cooked, grilled, fried, and fired! Our objective is to secure Luis Reinhart. Everything else will fall into place," I say.

"We need to sleep on it," Dewalt contests.

"Waiting is never a good strategy," Martini retorts.

"Luis will make it through the night," I reassure.

"What makes you believe he isn't dead?" Martini asks.

"Whoever is responsible needs Luis alive otherwise they wouldn't be coming after us. What time is it?" I inquire.

Agent Martini looks down at his watch, "10:30 p.m."

"Thank you. Send me the report on Ramona and rendezvous here in seven hours. When the docks open we take our chance," I decide.

"See you in seven hours sharp," Martini replies, heading for his suburban.

Detective Dewalt nods as we head to my vehicle. Agent Martini is gone and I am heading in the opposite direction. Classical jazz music plays while driving. Detective Dewalt remains quiet as I bring him home.

"Please, experience a good night's rest. Visit your family before we go through with our plans," I say.

"Don't patronize me Reisen," Dewalt snickers. "You aren't sure what will happen. I understand."

"Don't be selfish," I bemoan. "I want nothing more than to see Bonnie before we end up going off the deep end."

"Admirable behavior. Bonnie is a gem. Don't ever let her go. Not lofting Captain Davis in the mix is disingenuous."

Parallel parking in front of Detective Dewalt's duplex.

"Your briefcase is in the backseat," I say.

"Take good care of it," he replies.

Detective Dewalt muscles out of the car and up a flight of steps. Glancing back at me before opening his front door and entering inside. Inside of my hard outer shell, I feel his wife and family being overjoyed he's home.

Fire Burns Brighter After Midnight

Submitting my report on Ramona's homicide before departing. Detective Dewalt is unsure of tomorrow as am I.

Heading for Bonnie in a rush. A feeling of discontent erupts. I need her guidance and she deserves my affection. Maybe our last night of perfection.

Wrapped in each other's arms as we kiss. Lost in the shimmer of her eyes—wanting our love to endure the night. Words can't describe this shining delight. Kissing until we land on the mattress. Pulling the string on the light, I lust after her. Feeling divine as pressing matters slowly become benign.

Passion growing fiercer with each touch. Every muscle fiber twitching while our legs are kicking. Our aches heal as our bodies are flush with satisfaction. She is my shield and I am her sword. Darkness evaporates as our love won't exasperate.

A new horizon breaks as I awake. Forgoing an alarm for my internal clock. Making coffee in the kitchen not far from the master bedroom.

Bonnie's beauty infused in the sheets. She rolls over and smiles at me. A grand rising; feeling our signs were aligned. My spirit is revitalized with her by my side.

Sitting on the bed locking lips. Slowly feeling the back of her head. Gazing deep into her eyes, she bites my lips as a surprise.

"Something is bothering you. I can sense it," she speculates.

"Today is do or die," I say.

"Don't fret, sugar." Tenderly kissing me while grabbing my hands and placing them under hers, "Look how far you have come since this began."

Bonnie's eyes glow like fireflies in a mason jar as she yearns for the root cause of my dilemma. In our weakest moments, we learn where our allegiances lie. Ice-breaking into the ocean is the equivalent of our blossoming love.

Recent memories of Detective Dewalt's accident churn my stomach. Agent Martini and I bear witness to death's touch. Strife taken in stride never bolstering a long run wherever there's a badge and a gun.

Emotion fuels me while Bonnie ignites the fire in me. Lighting the logic lamp in my dark empty hive mind. Craving more—needing more—this is the life I desire. Regardless of how dark the road has become no shadow can stop a true man of God.

Hugging Bonnie, kissing her, and sliding away. "I will be back tonight. Will you be joining me for dinner?" I ask.

"If you let me decide what I want to eat."

"There is nothing I'd rather see than you figuring out your order before my food goes cold."

Kissing and hugging Bonnie tightly. Wrapped in a twister of detriment, benevolence, and rage.

"Please, be careful," she whispers.

"All day long!"

Slipping on my coat while grabbing my hat, and keys. Filling my thermos as one thought continues burning in my mind. Detective Dewalt wants me to contact Captain Davis. However, I haven't heard from him since my last near-death experience.

My risk tolerance is limited as I close in on Luis Reinhart's whereabouts. Gazing out the window while the engine warms up. Droplets of rain splash on the hood of the car as I flick on the windshield wipers. Foot on the gas pedal—heading for Detective Dewalt's residence.

Feeling someone over my shoulder as I fasten my mirror. A figure rises in the backseat. Slamming my breaks and skidding across the road.

"Whoa!" he yells, clutching both seats behind me as we come to a full stop.

None other than Captain Davis is along for the ride. Lighting up a cigar as he studies me. "Can I sit in the front? Wouldn't want ashes falling on your leather seats." Scooting out of the car before I respond. "Much better," Davis murmurs, reclining back in the passenger seat.

"I'm glad one of us is comfortable," I say as my heart rate subsides.

"Thought you wondered where I went after that lady tried knocking you off," Davis assumes. Puffing on his cigar as I resume driving.

"Did you read my report?" I ask, a tad irritated.

"I did. The report was well-typed. A woman posing as a police officer—pointed her weapon at you. Agent Martini discharged his firearm and saved your life," Davis details.

"That's my story and I'm sticking to it!"

"Everything checks out ... except one tiny detail."

"What detail would that be?" I inquire.

"How was impostor Ramona able to pass as a police officer in front of me and everyone else?"

"You are capable of finding out," I encourage.

"Way ahead of you! After digging, turns out Ramona worked on Mayor Riley's campaign," Davis reveals.

Utterly flabbergasted. "Someone is trying to send a message and Luis Reinhart is in more trouble than I first imagined."

"All the more reason you won't mind me tagging along."

"As a matter of fact; you are right where I want you."

Parallel parking in front of Detective Dewalt's duplex.

"Picking up Detective Dewalt?" Davis asks.

"How do you know?"

"I have to know," he replies.

The fog is rolling in thick. "Do you see him?" I ask.

"How can you see—"

Captain Davis's face runs long but doesn't flinch at the sight of Detective Dewalt gimping toward us. A navy blue lockbox with gold handles bounces off his left crutch.

"I see him ... it stings," Davis says.

Detective Dewalt favors one crutch and opens the door pulling himself into the back seat. "You finally took my advice," Dewalt mentions.

"Let's say your advice sprung up on me," I joke.

We all laugh as I begin driving. Captain Davis grins knowing we are speaking about him.

"Dewalt, I don't mean to be crude but how can you be of service in your present condition?" Davis inquires.

"Allow me to answer your question with a question of my own ... does a coffin benefit a dead man?" Dewalt asks.

Captain Davis's face shows a look of paralysis. Fixing my rear-view mirror noticing Detective Dewalt easing back in his seat.

"Where are we headed?" Davis asks, slicing the tension.

"A few more blocks. Agent Martini knows where to rendezvous," I explain.

"Since we are all present, allow me to lead the debriefing," Davis states. "After doing my best to delay the press from muddying up our affairs, if we uncover nothing; kiss our jobs goodbye!"

Absorbing Captain Davis's lambasting like a sponge. Taking a shortcut, time is short and might be cut shorter.

Media coverage would relish over a missing mayoral candidate ahead of a special election. Burying our task force while we buried Alderman Luis Reinhart.

Glancing at Detective Dewalt in the rear-view mirror as I change lanes. "What's in the lockbox?" I ask.

"You will see when we arrive at our destination."

The sun is rising as rain clouds do their best to cover the glare—glimmering across Lake Michigan.

"You have trusted me this far. Do you still trust me, Captain?" I ask.

"Reisen, you're a true *badge in the shadows.*"

Plotting on how to gain the upper hand. Pulling into the dirt road leading up the cliff. Struck by the muck as my tires sink into the ground.

"Stuck in the mud. That's a bad omen," Dewalt says.

"No. This is a sign sealed with promise," Davis retorts.

Agent Martini patiently looms. Coming to a halt and we exit.

"You're here! Brought a friend with you as well," Martini says.

"I'm Captain Davis of Progressive Task Force Twelve Z. Nice to meet you."

"I'm Agent Martini from the Criminal Intelligence Agency, pleasure is mine. Oh, I recall seeing you on television when your task force began. This isn't a simple extraction anymore," Martini heckles, shaking hands with Captain Davis.

"I don't plan on complicating matters more than they already are," Davis snorts.

"You know what ... I like how you roll," Martini snickers.

"If I may be of service," Dewalt starts.

Opening the lockbox. Holding up blueprints of what appears to be a layout marked with coordinates.

"How do you come across a novelty such as this?" I ask.

"My brother-in-law is an architect. He oversaw this project funded by Jake Frunk and loaned me the schematics," Dewalt finishes.

"Great work, Dewalt," Davis says, patting him on the back.

"Let's not get carried away. We must plan accordingly," Martini hisses.

"We are all justified in being here," I say. Studying the schematics. "Agent Martini, you enter from the west wing. Park your truck a quarter mile down the road. Pull in toward the water like you are fishing. Walk up the shoreline and sneak in." I direct. Pointing to the building's west side bordering the docks.

"Sounds doable," Martini confirms.

"Captain Davis, you roll with me. We enter on the eastern front. Stairs will be inside the hangar complex around the corner from the side door," I explain, running my finger across the schematic.

"Dewalt you take the binoculars and position yourself on the edge of the cliffs. You will be our eyes!" I declare.

Agent Martini walks over to the cliff and sets up a Beretta M107 sniper rifle.

"Count me in," Dewalt decides, positioning the weapon.

"Our chance of being axed increases the longer we are inside," Davis cautions.

"Then we've reached an accord. Agent Martini, when you are inside crawl through the ventilation system," I direct.

"You expect me to fit in a vent?" Martini asks.

All of us chuckle. "I wouldn't choose you if I didn't believe you could fit," I reassure.

"Thanks for considering my well-being," Martini crows.

Brushing off his comments. "You will be on the strong side of our enemies; meaning don't rush," I stress.

Detective Dewalt slides over and places his fingers on the blueprint, "There aren't a lot of places Luis can be. Search thoroughly."

Captain Davis looks as if he wants to speak, "Reisen, I will be frank. You've had the reigns but I have one final request."

"This should be interesting," Martini jibs.

"Please, ask." I encourage.

"Unless we die nobody better call for help."

Our faces shrink. "Are you mad?" Martini asks.

"Any particular reason why?" Dewalt inquires.

"I'd rather die in this heap as a martyr than made a mockery for what will surely come if we turn up empty-handed," Davis says prophetically—gradually washing away the tension.

"I happily grant your request. Death will surely be an acquired taste today," I acknowledge.

Detective Dewalt passes out small radios from the lockbox. "We need a secure frequency; set it to channel four."

We synchronize our radios.

Martini snaps the chamber shut on his revolver. "Only task left is pulling off a daring rescue," he declares, heading toward his suburban.

Captain Davis heads for my vehicle when Detective Dewalt pulls me to the side. "Earlier you said, 'we had to believe we would find Luis alive,'" Dewalt states.

"Don't worry—"

"I believe Luis is alive," Dewalt confesses, heading for the sniper rifle.

Organized Chaos

Pulling up near the entrance noticing trucks stationed for loading. Parking out of sight from the string of windows on the main building. Allowing trees and trucks to shield us.

Glancing at Captain Davis as I shut the engine off, "We jump over the concrete barrier and move behind the furthest truck on the right. We will shoot up the stairs after the coast is clear," I direct.

"What about the fence?"

"I will get us in. Might be a tight fit," I reply.

Captain Davis nods as we exit heading for the tall fence. Feeling confident with the blueprints pictured in my mind.

Carefully heating a spot on the fence with a blowtorch and slicing the metal open. Clearing enough space for us to crawl through.

Moving cautiously behind each truck. Peering at the open garages bordering Lake Michigan—where Agent Martini will appear.

Let's ease ourselves in without causing a commotion.

"Hey! Get out of here!" A voice demands.

Meeting the *chilling* stare of a driver in his truck.

Captain Davis and I pull him down—covering his mouth with my palm. "What's your name?" I ask.

Giving him air, "Fred!" he shrieks.

"Let me make your life simple, Fred. Take us to the rage room where you are holding our friend or so help me *God, I will bring the law down on you as the Lord did to the Egyptians*," I demand.

"I will show you inside if you let me go after," he pleads.

"If your luck doesn't run out first!" Davis barks.

Nearing the side door, dragging Fred along.

"If anybody asks, you are taking us on a tour," I say.

Moving ahead of Captain Davis who is behind Fred. Checking every angle remaining unseen. Motioning for Fred and Captain Davis to pick up the pace.

"If you make any trouble you won't be spared," Davis taunts, shoving Fred ahead.

Carrying on along the second floor as we place ourselves against opposite sides of a steel frame.

"Time to boogie down. Open up and escort your friends inside," Davis demands.

My attentiveness wouldn't allow me to laugh. Fred leads us into a utility room with doors going two different ways. Stairs going up the sidewall lay ahead as the blueprint indicated. Spotting a wide array of fuel tanks and cleaning supplies.

"Up the stairs we go," I say.

"Alright, where am I taking you?" Fred asks.

"Work and talk," Davis growls.

Fred's complexion unravels as we ascended.

"Where would you keep a man if he must be hidden?" I inquire.

"Usually a break room," Fred heckles.

Halting Fred in his tracks and shoving him against the wall, "Don't let the badge fool you. Shadows will swarm and swallow everything you are involved in if you make another dumb remark."

"I don't know anything about a man being hidden here."

"I didn't ask for cockiness. Where would you keep a man if he needs to be hidden?"

Fred is shivering—his lips blubbering, "... I might know a place," he gulps.

"You need to know and you need to show us."

Briskly sweeping Fred through the door. Barging in a narrow hallway with an empty office corridor on the left of us. Railing on the right of us with stairs going down. A sharp turn lay ahead if we didn't take the stairs.

"Keep moving and keep it down," I order.

All of us hunch down shuffling toward the fork in our path. Time to choose our destiny.

"How do we act?" Davis whispers.

"You heard him, Fred," I say, nudging him.

"Be easy," he says rubbing his shoulder. "The only place a person can be hidden is downstairs and in the storm shelter."

"After you," I say motioning forward toward the stairs.

Making our way down the stairs. On the ground sticking close behind Captain Davis with Fred walking in-between us. Casually looking behind for any onlookers. A grave feeling of someone watching hasn't escaped me.

Whipping around the corner, hearing a truck starting up and pulling out. Lucky for us we are out of the driver's view. We follow the wall leading us to double doors.

"Do we go in here?" Davis asks.

"Yes," Fred squeaks.

Entering and shutting the doors behind us. Surveying the room—white painted brick walls with one window fitted in the corner. Unable to determine if Detective Dewalt would have a clear shot if we are compromised. Using the radio and my cell phone to no avail.

"No phone service. What kind of place is this?" Davis asks.

"Was designed as a storm shelter back in 1929," Fred explains.

"Is this room in use?" I ask.

"Functioning but supposedly put out of service eons ago," Fred says.

In the corner parallel to the window on the floor lies a latch.

Slinging the hatch open, "Time to find out," I say.

Captain Davis, Fred, and I descend into the depths below. Initially, the room is spacious.

"Captain, you lead," I direct.

"You are out of your minds!" Fred howls.

"Enough out of you! Get moving!" Davis barks.

Fred proceeds behind Captain Davis. Passing bars on the wall as our path draws short and narrow. Peering ahead over their backs.

Hearing a thunderous thud. "Hurry!" I shout.

We hustle forward forced to hit our knees; doing mountain climbers until the last turn where we can stand. ... The scene poisons my spirit.

Fred pukes as we are dumbfounded. Alderman Luis Reinhart lays battered with his feet and hands bound. His mouth duck taped shut. Left to die at the hands of savages!

Peeling the tape off Luis's lips as his eyes open. "You ... found me."

"Cut him loose and bring him up carefully," Davis orders.

Fred and I sit Luis up. "We have to get out of here," he coughs.

"I had no idea—," Fred starts before I cut him off.

Tackling Fred down ready to lay into him as he shields his face but I hold back—painfully staring him down.

"He isn't in on this Reisen," Luis assures, dry heaving.

I let go of Fred and pull him to his feet. Captain Davis finishes slicing the rope bonding Luis's feet.

"Can you move your legs?" Davis asks.

"Yes. Help me up," Luis says holding out both of his arms.

Pulling him up, and embracing him while fighting back tears.

"Let's hurry out of here," Davis says.

"I owe you a solid, old friend. Thank you, everyone," Luis emphasizes.

"Harder entering this bottomless pit than leaving," Davis says. Flinging open the hatch and we all ascend.

The double doors swing open, "That's far enough!" Agent Martini's pistol is drawn.

A guest accompanies him. I recognize her quickly as Mayor Riley.

"This is how low you've stooped?" I ask, disheartened.

"You are all here without a warrant. Simply, leave Luis with us and take your absence. This will all disappear," Riley says.

"What's wrong Mayor Riley? Are you bitter?" Luis asks as I hold him up.

"You won't get away with this! Madame Mayor, you disgust me!" Davis laments, spitting on the ground.

"Don't lecture me, Captain Davis! "Feel blessed I don't have your head," Riley scolds.

"They don't need a warrant—I brought them in." Fred blurts.

Martini fires a shot from his gun; ringing out like a bell as the bullet leaves the compensated barrel. Fred falls to his side and dies.

Mayor Riley's expression turns ghastly, "You said, 'there wouldn't be any killing!'"

"Wasn't up to me," Martini replies.

"It's all up to you," I say.

Captain Davis draws his pistol but Agent Martini beats him to the punch; wounding him. Dropping his firearm falling to the floor shouting in agony.

"Get me out of here!" Riley shouts, barging out of the door.

"Drop your weapon, Reisen! I will clean up the mess!" Martini demands.

I drop my firearm and kick it over to him. Agent Martini leans down and scoops up my weapon. "Good work—"

Agent Martini is interrupted by shattering glass. A bullet strikes his skull. He slumps down; raising his weapon at me. Dying before pulling the trigger. Hard to tell with Martini's eyes open but I feel his soul vacate the premises.

Stunned while picking up my firearm. Checking on Captain Davis. He has a pulse but is passed out from shock. Workers gather near the doorway. A woman screams and some folks cry.

"Call an ambulance!" Wrapping my shirt around Captain Davis's bullet wound and applying pressure.

After a few moments, we hear sirens. I feel Captain Davis grip my arm. "I told you Detective Dewalt came from good water." Wincing in pain while he cracks a smile.

"Glad I brought you along. Paramedics are almost here." Attempting to comfort him.

"You may not be a hero but you sure put on a good front," Davis coughs.

Full of merriment and pain, "That's the only compliment you have ever given me," I say.

"The only compliment you will get out of me," Davis says.

Alderman Luis Reinhart sits parallel to us. "I don't know about good water. However, I know something about water," Luis implies.

"What do you know about water?" I inquire.

"Detective Reisen, you come from the fountain of youth."

We chuckle while gritting our teeth. Captain Davis reaches in his pocket pulling out a blood-stained warrant. Tossing the crumpled piece of paper on Agent Martini's dead body as paramedics carry Captain Davis and Alderman Luis Reinhart away.

What Now?

Regrouping with Detective Dewalt at his residence.

"What did we learn today?" I ask.

"I see things coming quicker than you do," Dewalt hisses.

Putting Detective Dewalt in a headlock and giving him a noogie.

"I am joking," Dewalt whines as I let him go.

"I learned you are a well-rounded partner," I declare, giving him a fist bump.

"You aren't too shabby," he snickers. "The next noogie will turn into fisticuffs," Dewalt warns.

Shadow-boxing while Detective Dewalt seems uninterested. "I forgot you know how to fight," I scoff. "What are your plans for tonight?"

"Strictly business but first comes love," Dewalt replies.

"Are you interested in a double date tonight?" I ask.

"I'll think about it," Dewalt responds, heading for his motorcycle.

"Since we aren't keeping secrets. I have one to get off my chest," I begin.

Stopping and turning his head around. "I'm listening."

"Do you know how we became partners?" I inquire.

"A stroke of luck," Dewalt jokes.

"I was clocking in when you broke up a fight between two police officers. How you handled the situation showed your character. I knew you would become my partner but I never guessed you would save my life," I reveal.

"We saved each other," Dewalt says as he departs.

Meeting Bonnie at the door when I arrive home. She is sobbing as we embrace—our love sparks the rest of the day.

"Do you want breakfast for dinner?" I ask.

"Be better in bed," Bonnie replies.

Kissing—hugging—sensing dark clouds removing themselves. Taking our sweet time freshening up.

Heading for good eats and then a nice retreat. Bonnie is by my side. *Praying for a smooth ride.*

Pulling in front of Big Clark's Diner. Opening Bonnie's door and escorting her inside. Fetching a table my emotions are stable as I spot a familiar face.

"Hey!" Kimberly shouts. "Let's start you two love birds out with some drinks," she says.

Same face but her hair is lined with pink streaks. A shadow hides what appears to be a pineapple tattoo on her neckline.

"We're ready to order!" Bonnie declares.

"Great! What will you have dear?" Kimberly asks.

Bonnie folds her menu down, "Rib tips and barbecue fries."

I raise my hand to object, "I thought we were going with breakfast for dinner."

"Of course! French toast on the side and a glass of pink lemonade please," Bonnie retorts.

Sitting back in my booth, "I'll have Eggs Benedict and a coffee." Winking at Bonnie.

Big Clark's Diner is nearly empty. A few patrons line the counter sitting on yellow spinning stools. The door swings open and Detective Dewalt and his wife enter. Recognizing Bonnie and me. Dewalt ushers his wife to our booth.

"This is my wife Caroline. May we join you?" Dewalt asks.

"I'd be insulted if you didn't," I reply. Standing up hugging them both, Bonnie follows suit.

Epilogue

Alderman Luis Reinhart wins the special election in a nail-biter. Going on record as the closest mayoral race in Chicago's history. Newspaper reporters are at full strength invoking a media spectacle. Leaving the television set off for nearly a month after seeing my face blasted every day.

The toxicology report came back on Judge Marshall. His cause of death was food poisoning. Mayor-Elect Luis Reinhart is no longer a suspect. What bothers me most of all is the shadow driver in front of Big Clark's Diner never reappeared and that is no secret.

Detective Dewalt is happy with his family, ready for his next assignment, and anxious to retire his crutches. We must wait and see if former Mayor Riley will be prosecuted and that weighs on my conscious along with the loss of my dear friend, Agent Martini.

Captain Davis is in a sling but remains his youthful self. Surgeons were able to remove the bullet from Davis's arm. A relief he will survive to tell the undesirable story for ages. He is on the money about one thing, Chicago needs a hero. Unsure whether I am deserving but certain I am returning.

Afterword

A fragment of a hero lies inside us. We become the villain or savior of the moment. When opportunity knocks and your hidden power is awakened a righteous path will starve off wrath.

Don't miss out!

Visit the website below and you can sign up to receive emails whenever Preston Olson publishes a new book. There's no charge and no obligation.

https://books2read.com/r/B-A-XTTR-YFDZB

BOOKS2READ

Connecting independent readers to independent writers.